FALKIRK COMMUNITY TRUST

30124 02

D0727395

GASP OF THE
GHOULISH GUINEA PIG

For my super-cool nephews Quinten
and Elliot – SH

For Gizmo, our fine, furry friend – SC

STRIPES PUBLISHING
An imprint of Little Tiger Press
1 The Coda Centre, 189 Munster Road,
London SW6 6AW

A paperback original
First published in Great Britain in 2014

Text copyright © Sam Hay, 2014
Illustrations copyright © Simon Cooper, 2014

ISBN: 978-1-84715-423-1

The right of Sam Hay and Simon Cooper to be identified as the author
and illustrator of this work respectively has been asserted by them in
accordance with the Copyright, Designs and Patents Act, 1988.

All rights reserved.

A CIP catalogue record for this book is available from
the British Library.

This book is sold subject to the condition that it shall not, by
way of trade or otherwise, be lent, resold, hired out, or otherwise
circulated without the publisher's prior consent in any form of
binding or cover other than that in which it is published and
without a similar condition, including this condition, being
imposed upon the subsequent purchaser.

Printed and bound in the UK.
10 9 8 7 6 5 4 3 2 1

Falkirk Council	
Askews & Holts	2013
JF JF	£4.99

UNDEAD PETS

GASP OF THE GHOULISH GUINEA PIG

SAM HAY

ILLUSTRATED BY
SIMON COOPER

Stripes

The story so far...

Ten-year-old Joe Edmunds is desperate for a pet.

But his mum's allergies mean that he's got no chance.

Then his great-uncle Charlie gives him an ancient Egyptian amulet that he claims will grant Joe a single wish...

But instead of getting a pet, Joe becomes the Protector of Undead Pets. He is bound by the amulet to solve the problems of zombie pets so they can pass peacefully to the afterlife.

CHAPTER ONE

"Here they come!" called Joe.

Toby, his little brother, gave a squeal of delight as a streak of brown and white fur shot out of a bendy green tube, closely followed by two more.

"Go, guinea pigs!" shouted Erin, a curly-haired girl the same age as Joe. She was sitting at the other end of the hall waving a bunch of parsley, while three guinea pigs raced through the obstacle course towards her, squeaking as they went.

UNDEAD PETS

It was Sunday afternoon, the start of the half-term holiday, and Joe and Toby and their parents were visiting the Crawfords. While the grown-ups chatted in the living room, the children were playing with the family's three guinea pigs – Lightning, Flash and Bolt. The obstacle course they'd built ran down the length of the Crawfords' hallway.

"Oops!" giggled George, Erin's little brother, as the guinea pigs decided not to jump over the small fence they'd made and went round the side instead.

"They're heading for the seesaw!" shrieked Toby.

"Come on!" called Erin, waving the parsley up and down. "Come and get the goodies!"

Flash – the biggest guinea pig – sniffed the air and let out a squeak of excitement, then shot through the cardboard archway and over the finish line, closely followed by Bolt and Lightning.

"Why does Flash always win?" groaned George.

"Because he's awesome!" Erin scooped Flash up gently and rewarded him with a sprig of parsley. "That's why I chose him."

"Lightning and Bolt are cool, too," said George, giving the other two their share of the parsley.

Joe crouched down next to Erin and stroked Flash's small brown and white head. "When did you get them?"

"About four months ago. They're still quite young…"

"And very excitable!" added Erin's mum, who had appeared in the hall carrying a tray of empty mugs. "All that squeaking!"

"Squeak! Squeak!" mimicked George in a funny guinea-pig voice.

Toby giggled and joined in. "Squeak! Squeak! Squeak!"

The guinea pigs stopped chewing their parsley and looked at the boys as though they were mad.

"I wish I had a guinea pig," sighed Toby. "They're so cool."

"Want to hold Flash?" Erin nodded to the space next to her. "Sit there and I'll put him on your lap. Watch out – he's a bit of a pooper!"

Toby and George giggled.

"Can I hold one, too?" Joe asked.

George put Bolt on Joe's knee. The guinea pig began snuffling around his pockets looking for treats. Joe stroked his head and the guinea pig gave a small squeak.

"He likes you," said Erin.

But just then Bolt wriggled off Joe's lap and scuttled back to Lightning.

"They're best friends," George explained. "They like to stick together."

"What about Flash?" asked Joe. The biggest guinea pig was still sitting happily on Toby's knee.

"He's a bit braver," said Erin. "The other two follow him about. It's a bit like me and George," she giggled. "I'm Flash and George is Bolt!"

"Joe, Toby – five minutes!" Mum called from the living room.

Toby groaned. "I don't want to go home!"

"Quick," Erin said. "Let's do the course again!" She picked up Flash and Lightning, while George took Bolt, and they carried them back to the beginning of the obstacle course.

As soon as Erin let Flash go, he took off through the first tunnel, squeaking excitedly.

"Hey!" said Erin, as Lightning wriggled in

UNDEAD PETS

her arms. She put him down and he chased after
Flash. Bolt caught up, following the others.

George and Toby began squeaking again,
copying the guinea pigs.

"We've got two new pets!" said Mrs Crawford
as the grown-ups appeared in the hall.

Joe's dad grinned. "Shall I put them in the
hutch for you?"

Toby and George made silly guinea-pig
faces and squeaked even louder.

"Come on, boys! Time to go," said Mum, holding out Toby's fleece.

Toby's face fell. "But I want to stay."

"You can come another time," said Mrs Crawford. "What about Tuesday? It's George's birthday and he's having a monster party. It would be lovely if Joe and Toby could come."

"Yes, please!" said Toby excitedly.

"Cool!" George added.

Joe was less enthusiastic. The idea of a five-year-old's birthday party wasn't so appealing to him.

"Well…" he began.

Mrs Crawford smiled. "Maybe you've already got plans, Joe. But it would be lovely if Toby could come."

"Are you sure you don't mind?" Mum asked Mrs Crawford.

"Of course not! We've already got a houseful of kids coming – another one won't matter."

"Awesome!" said Toby and George. And they started squeaking again.

"Five more minutes, Joe, and then turn it off!" called Dad, poking his head round the living-room door.

It was a few hours later and Joe was playing a motor-racing video game.

"Did you hear me?" Joe's dad asked.

Joe made a face. "Yeah, all right, Dad."

Just one more lap, he thought to himself as he steered his car through the flags.

Squeak! Squeak! Squeak!

"Get lost, Toby!" Joe grumbled, not bothering to turn round. "Dad says I've still got five minutes!"

Squeak! Squeak! Squeak!

"Go away!"

Squeak! Squeak! Squeak!

UNDEAD PETS

Why were little brothers so annoying! Joe grabbed a cushion, spun round and lobbed it at Toby – but he wasn't there.

Squeak! Squeak! Squeak!

Joe frowned. "Toby? Where are you?"

"Under here, Joe!" came a squeaky voice.

Joe peered under the coffee table and gasped. It was Flash!

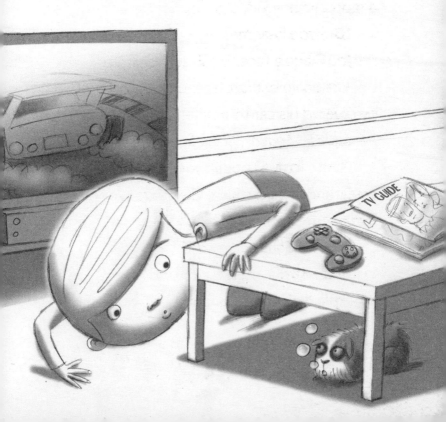

CHAPTER TWO

Joe blinked a few times. It really *was* Flash. But the guinea pig looked different to the super-sleek blur of fur that had been zooming round the obstacle course at the Crawfords' house earlier that day.

Flash's coat was damp. His eyes were big, green and staring. And every time he opened his mouth, little soapy bubbles popped out.

Joe rubbed his eyes.

"I need your help!" said Flash urgently, and an extra big bubble popped out of his nose, filling the room with a flowery smell.

Joe gulped. "Are you … er … dead?"

"I can't pass over properly until you help me!"

Joe groaned. Flash had become an Undead Pet, another creature stuck in limbo, unable to pass over to the afterlife until his problems had been solved. And thanks to the magical Egyptian amulet that his great-uncle Charlie had given him, there was only one person who could help – Joe!

"But, how…?" Joe muttered. "I was playing with you a few hours ago!"

"A lot has happened since you left," the guinea pig said miserably.

Just then there was a shout from upstairs.

"Come on, Joe," called Dad. "Turn it off now!"

"OK, coming!" Joe flicked the game off and turned back to Flash. "What happened to you?"

UNDEAD PETS

Flash trotted out from under the table, leaving a trail of damp footprints on the carpet. "It's a long story…"

The guinea pig gave himself a shake, splattering Joe with sweet-smelling droplets.

"Urgh! What's that smell? Did you pour a bottle of perfume over your head or something?"

"It's fabric softener," said Flash.

"What?"

"You know, the gloopy stuff that goes in the washing machine." As Flash spoke a ripple of bubbles escaped from his nose.

"But how did you get covered in it?"

"After you left, George and Erin

put us back in our hutch, but I wanted to keep playing. I noticed that George hadn't shut the hutch properly…"

"So you got out?" Joe asked.

Flash nodded. "I ran through the kitchen, but then something horrible appeared!" He began to shiver and a big bubble burst out of his left nostril.

"What was it?"

"A snake!" Flash let out a squeal.

"Very funny!" Joe rolled his eyes.

"No, really. There was a snake in the kitchen!" Flash's fur was standing on end now and his eyes bulged. "It was huge. A monster!"

Joe frowned. "But Erin and George don't have a snake."

"I saw it!" squeaked Flash.

"OK, then," said Joe, going along with the story, although he found it hard to believe. "What did you do?"

I froze. I was terrified!

Then I ran! I spotted the washing machine door was open.

There was a pile of clothes next to it. I climbed up and dived inside...

But then Mum came in. She didn't see me.

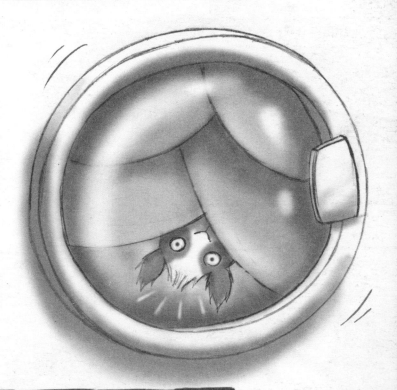

She stuffed the clothes inside the machine and turned it on!

Joe winced. "You drowned?"

Flash nodded. "Look at me!"

Joe popped a few bubbles as they drifted out of the damp guinea pig's mouth and floated towards him. "So, what do you need me for?"

"To save my friends from the snake! What if it eats Bolt and Lightning?"

"But maybe it wasn't a snake," Joe said. "I mean, snakes don't just pop up in kitchens. And I think the Crawfords would know if there *was* one hanging round their house. Maybe it was just a hose pipe or a skipping rope."

A stubborn expression appeared on Flash's face. "It *was* a snake! A huge one. And they won't know about it because it's hiding behind the fridge! I saw it slither off there when Mum came into the kitchen."

Joe scratched his head. "But how could a snake just sneak into someone's house without them seeing it?"

"I don't know! But you've got to stop it, Joe," Flash said firmly, "before it gobbles up my friends!"

CHAPTER THREE

Joe wasn't sure what to do next. He wanted to help Flash but he couldn't exactly call the Crawfords and tell them there was a snake in their kitchen. They'd never believe him. He still wasn't sure he believed it himself!

"Come on," he said. "Maybe we can find out what sort of snake you *think* you saw."

"Hey!" squealed the guinea pig as Joe picked him up and squashed him into the large front pocket of his hoodie.

Joe crept out into the hall and listened.

He could hear Toby splashing about in the bath upstairs. Dad was talking to him. He could hear Mum up there, too, moving around. Luckily, he didn't have to worry about Sarah – his pain-in-the-neck big sister was away at Guide Camp.

Joe snuck into the kitchen and spotted Dad's new tablet computer lying on the table. He lifted Flash out of his pocket, then switched on the tablet and tapped in the word "snake".

"What colour was it?" asked Joe.

"Orange!"

"And how big was it?"

"Enormous!" gasped Flash.

Joe smiled. "Yeah, but everything looks enormous to you, Flash, because you're so little!"

Flash made an indignant snorting noise and a stream of bubbles burst out of his nose. "It was nearly as long as this table!"

"Really?" Joe reckoned the kitchen table was about a metre long. If there really *was* a snake, then it was a big one! He tapped in the details.

Joe spotted a site about exotic pets in the search results. He opened the page and then clicked on a photo of an orange snake. "There!" he pointed. "Is that it?"

Flash peered at the picture of the snake and gave a squeal. "That's it!"

Joe read the text. "It's a corn snake," he said. "It says they're not dangerous to people…"

"But what about guinea pigs?"

Joe read some more. "Oh."

"What? What is it, Joe?"

"It says corn snakes should be kept away from other pets … and…"

"What?" Flash peered up at Joe. "Tell me!"

"Well, it says that a corn snake's main source of food is … small rodents!"

Flash gave a super-loud squeak and a rush of bubbles popped out of his ears, filling the air with flowery scent.

UNDEAD PETS

"Joe?"

Mum was standing in the doorway. "What are you doing? And what's that smell? Have you been spraying air freshener?"

"No!" Joe shook his head. "It's nothing to do with me!"

Mum gave her nose a rub. She couldn't see the undead pets – no one apart from Joe could. But thanks to her allergies she could always sense when one was close.

"Why are you using Dad's tablet?" Mum asked. "You know he said you had to get permission."

Joe felt his face turn red. "I was just finding out about … animals."

Mum sighed. "I know how much you love animals, and I could see that you and Toby had a great time playing with the guinea pigs, but we've been through this hundreds of times! We can't have a pet because of my allergies."

"But you didn't sneeze so much today, Mum. Maybe guinea pigs don't bother you like other animals do."

"No, it's because I took an allergy pill. But the medicine doesn't make my allergies disappear altogether. In fact," she wrinkled her nose and blinked a few times, "it must be wearing off. My nose actually feels a bit tickly now…" She gave her eyes a rub. "Turn off the tablet now, please, Joe." She turned and left the room.

Joe waited until she'd gone then looked back at the screen. "I just want to check one more thing…" He tapped in the words "escaped snake" then hit enter.

"Wow!" he breathed. There were hundreds of stories about people finding escaped snakes in their houses. Perhaps Flash's story wasn't as mad as he'd thought! Joe clicked on one story and a picture of a giant python lying on a bathroom radiator appeared.

Joe could hear his mum calling him again. He scooped up Flash and headed for the door.

"What are we going to do now?" Flash squeaked.

"I'm sure I'll think of something," whispered Joe, climbing into bed later that night. "Maybe I could go round to the Crawfords' house in the morning and try and find the snake…"

Flash sighed. "If it's not already too late."

Joe placed Flash in an old shoebox stuffed with socks then lay down and flicked his bedside light off.

A moment later he felt something cold and soggy wriggling by his feet. The next second, Flash popped his head out from under the duvet on to Joe's pillow.

"Guinea pigs stick together," squeaked Flash, nuzzling up to Joe.

"But I'm not a guinea pig!" Joe grimaced. "Budge up!" he added crossly. But Flash was already asleep, snoring bubbles.

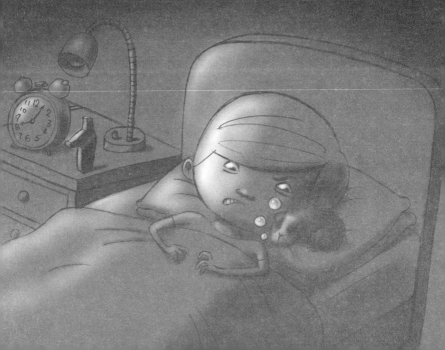

CHAPTER FOUR

The next morning, Toby was standing in his pyjamas, watching Joe put on his trainers.

"Where are you going?" Toby asked.

"Out!" said Joe. He was trying not to squish Flash as he leaned over. The guinea pig was tucked inside his hoodie pocket again. "On my bike!"

"Why?"

"Because I want to."

"But we're going bowling today," said Toby, who had slipped on Dad's shoes and was clumping about in the hallway next to Joe.

Joe groaned. He'd forgotten that he was supposed to be meeting his mates Matt and Ben at the bowling alley.

Joe glanced at the clock. "That's not until later. Eleven o'clock, wasn't it? I'm going out on my bike first. See you!"

Joe slipped out of the front door before Dad appeared.

"I hope we're not too late," squeaked Flash, popping his pink nose out and sniffing the morning air. "The snake might have got them already!"

"I doubt it," muttered Joe. "Or I'd have had two more undead pets in my bed this morning!" He fetched his bike from the side of the house and climbed on. "I hope the Crawfords let me in."

The plan was to cycle over to the Crawfords' house and pretend he'd left his cap there.

I wonder whether they'll remember I wasn't

actually wearing a cap yesterday, Joe thought.

As they hurtled down Joe's road, Flash let out an excited squeal. "Faster, Joe!"

Less than five minutes later, they were outside the Crawfords' house. Joe took a deep breath and pressed the doorbell. He shuffled impatiently, his confidence disappearing.

Flash wriggled out of Joe's pocket. "I'll sneak inside and take a look."

He scrambled down Joe's leg and disappeared straight through the front door.

Joe rang the bell again.

"They're out, loser!"

Joe spun round to find Spiker – the most annoying boy in his class – smirking at him from the garden next door.

"What are you doing here?" Joe spluttered.

"I live here!"

"What?"

Spiker rolled his eyes and nodded to the

house next door to the Crawfords'. "That's mine, dimwit!" Then his eyes narrowed. "What are *you* doing here?"

Before Joe could answer, a smug smile appeared on Spiker's face. "Are you Erin's boyfriend?"

"No!"

"Joe loves Erin!" Spiker sang.

Joe felt his face turn beetroot red. "Get lost!"

UNDEAD PETS

"Wait till I tell everyone at school!"

"No!"

Just then, Flash reappeared through the wall of the Crawfords' house. "They're out, Joe. I saw a window open at the back of the house. Sneak inside so you can hunt for the snake!"

Joe frowned. Even if Spiker hadn't been there, no way was he going to break into someone's house!

"Talk to me, Joe!" squealed Flash. "What's the plan?" He scrabbled anxiously at Joe's ankles, scratching him through his socks. "Do something!"

Joe gave Flash an exasperated look. Didn't he understand they were being watched? He bent down and pretended to retie his shoelace. "We'll come back later!" he hissed.

"Want me to tell Erin you came round?" shouted Spiker.

"What?"

"I'll tell her you send your LOVE!" Spiker made a soppy face.

"GET LOST!" Joe scooped up Flash, stuffed him back in his pocket and headed for his bike.

"No!" Angry bubbles exploded from Flash's nose. "What about my friends? Guinea pigs stick together!"

Joe didn't answer. As he got on his bike, he expected Spiker to tease him again. But he didn't. Spiker's back was turned and he appeared to be looking for something in the bushes.

"Strike!" Matt shouted.

"Wow! You're on fire! High five!" Ben leaped up to slap palms with Matt.

The bowling alley was packed full of families enjoying the half-term holiday.

Joe heard another yelp of delight from the lane next to them and watched Toby and his friend Ricky high-fiving, too.

"Even my little brother's doing better than me," Joe muttered.

Flash was scuttling round Joe's feet non-stop. "When can we go, Joe?" he was squeaking. "I'm worried – so worried."

The more Joe thought about the snake, the more anxious he felt. He could just picture the snake slithering across the kitchen, inching towards the guinea pigs…

"Strike!" yelled Ben, punching the air.

"Awesome!" Matt slapped Ben on the back. "But I'm still beating you."

"Only just!" Ben replied.

Both boys looked at Joe. It was his turn next.

Joe ran his hands over all the bowling balls and grasped a big purple one that was really too big for him, but looked impressive!

He staggered to the lane.

"Want me to get a strike for you, Joe?" Ben teased.

Joe shot him a glare then lunged forward, aiming as straight as he could. The weight of the ball made him lurch sideways and he dropped it on to the lane heavily.

The ball began rolling slowly towards the pins.

Matt snorted and Ben stifled a giggle.

Eventually the ball drifted left and dropped into the gutter.

"Unlucky, Joe!" called Dad from the next lane. "Try a lighter ball!"

"Maybe you need the rubber buffers, too," giggled Matt. "Like the little kids have!"

Joe scowled.

"Sorry, mate," Matt said. "Just kidding."

Joe grabbed another ball and stepped back on to the lane to bowl it. As he let go, Flash shot out from between his feet and zoomed down the lane in front of the ball.

"That looks better!" called Dad.

Joe's ball was much straighter this time, but it still lacked power – it certainly wasn't going fast enough to knock all the pins down.

BANG!

The ball slapped into the front pin. Three pins fell and a couple of others wobbled...

"Nah – you're not gonna get them all," said Matt. "Shame."

"Wait!" said Ben. "Look!"

More pins were falling.

Flash was streaking in and out, head-butting the pins. In seconds they were all down.

Ben and Matt stared.

"How did you do that?" Matt asked with a frown. Then he grinned. "High five!"

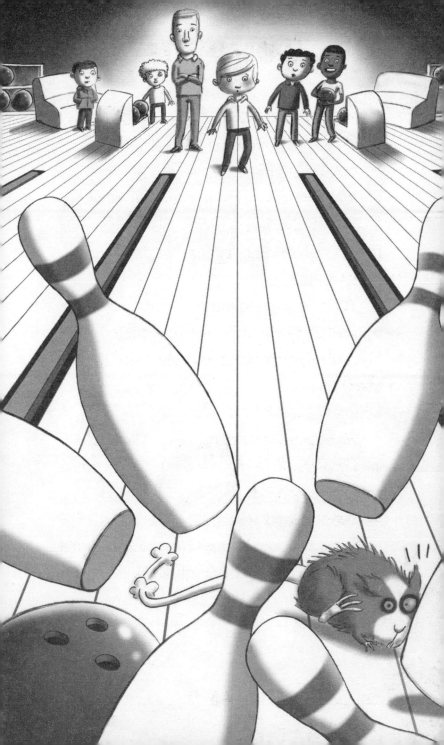

CHAPTER FIVE

"You were awesome, Joe!" said Toby as they got into the car to go home. "You smashed Matt and Ben!"

Flash gave a happy squeak. "Guinea pigs stick together!"

Joe grinned. For once he didn't mind being counted as a guinea pig. Thanks to Flash, Joe had won that game – and the one after. He'd even beaten his dad's score! Being Protector of Undead Pets had got Joe into many tricky situations so it made a change for one of the pets to actually do something to help him!

"Can we go for pizza?" Toby begged.

"Not today," said Dad. "But we are going to stop off at the shops on the way home. Mum asked us to pick up something for George's birthday. Any ideas?"

"Guinea pigs!" shouted Toby.

"What?" Joe jumped. Could Toby see Flash?

"Let's get George something for his guinea pigs – some toys or something…"

Phew! Joe thought.

"Good idea!" said Dad. "We'll go to the pet shop and have a look."

They pulled into a parking space.

"Don't worry," Joe whispered to Flash, putting the guinea pig back into his hoodie pocket. "It won't take long."

They got out of the car and Joe hung back behind Dad and Toby, pretending to fiddle with his watch. "Maybe the shop will have a book

UNDEAD PETS

about snakes," Joe whispered. "We might get some ideas for where to look."

"The snake's behind the fridge!" snapped Flash. "I told you!"

"Yeah, but it might not have stayed in the same place. If it did, I reckon the Crawfords would have spotted it by now."

Joe ran to catch up with Toby and Dad.

The pet shop was enormous.

"Joe!" called Toby. "Come and look at the guinea pigs!"

UNDEAD PETS

Flash gave an excited squeal. "Let me see, let me see!"

He scrambled down Joe's leg and hurtled after Toby, squeaking loudly.

Inside the pen was a gang of baby guinea pigs, munching hay. By the time Joe arrived, Flash was already in there, sniffing and nuzzling and making happy squeaky noises.

"Some of them are hiding!" said Toby, pointing to a pair of smaller guinea pigs that were peeking out from under a plastic pet house.

"They must be scared," chuckled Dad. "I would be, too, with your ugly mug staring at me!" He ruffled Toby's hair.

"Can we have one, Dad? Please!"

"Don't be silly, Toby. Come and choose some toys for George…"

Toby's shoulders slumped. Then he spotted another pen. "Wow! Rabbits!" he said, and raced over.

Joe lingered, looking at the guinea pigs. They were chasing each other round the pen now, with Flash joining in as though he was still alive.

Then Joe noticed a series of large tanks, right at the back of the room. He went over to take a closer look.

Two small geckos stared back at him out of the first tank, their tiny ink-spot eyes following his every movement. Joe went over to the next tank where a bright green chameleon sat on a log. The last tank was empty.

UNDEAD PETS

Joe was just about to go back to the chameleon when he felt a tap on his shoulder.

"Didn't see her, did you?" A young shop assistant was standing there with a cleaning spray in one hand and a bucket of soapy water in the other. She smiled at Joe. "She's good at hiding."

Joe peered into the last tank again. Finally he spotted a small stripey orange snake right at the back, half hidden under a curved piece of bark. It poked its tongue out at him. It was similar to the one he'd seen on the internet only much smaller – it looked like a shoelace.

"Is it a corn snake?" asked Joe.

"Yep, just a baby. She'll grow much, much bigger."

Joe glanced over his shoulder to make sure Dad and Toby weren't listening. "Do pet snakes ever escape?" he asked.

"Oh yeah! Lucky, my boa constrictor, got

out once. We tried all the tricks — laying out food, dusting the floors with flour to see if we could spot where she'd been… Then Mum found her at the back of the airing cupboard snuggled into the warm towels!"

Joe grinned. He could just imagine what would happen if his mum found a snake in their airing cupboard! "Where else do they hide?" he asked.

"Anywhere warm. Snakes hate the cold. Behind the fridge is another hiding place — the motor makes it hot there."

So that was why Flash saw the snake sneak behind the fridge! thought Joe.

"Down the back of the sofa," the girl went on, "under floorboards… Bigger snakes are quite strong. If you don't put a brick on top of the vivarium lid, they can push their way out! Are you thinking of getting one?"

Before Joe could answer there was a shout from the other side of the room. "Caitlin!" It was the pet-shop owner, calling from the cash desk. "Can you fetch a box of pinkies for this boy?"

Joe glanced over and gasped.

It was Spiker!

He hadn't noticed Joe yet. He was too busy counting out a pile of change.

"Gotta go!" the girl said, and she disappeared into the back of the shop.

Joe headed over to Dad and Toby, who were comparing guinea-pig toys. But as he passed the cash desk he heard Spiker talking to the pet-shop owner.

"And you reckon if I put out more snake food he'll come back?" Spiker asked.

Joe froze. Did he really just say "snake food"?

The man nodded. "Yep, if he's been missing for a few days, he's bound to get hungry soon. Just put some of his usual food — a couple of dead mice — near his tank. You can try other places, too. Corn snakes usually come back when they smell grub!"

Joe gasped. Spiker had lost a corn snake… And he lived next door to the Crawfords! That meant it was probably his snake that Flash had seen.

"What are you staring at?" Spiker growled, peering at Joe.

Joe shrugged. Then he had an idea. If he could somehow tempt the snake out of the

Crawfords' house and back to Spiker's then all his troubles would be over!

"Did you say you've lost a snake?" asked Joe.

"No!" Spiker glanced round nervously. "You heard wrong."

"Here you go!" said Caitlin, arriving with a cardboard box. "Remember to defrost them before you feed them to your snake, OK?"

Spiker's face went beetroot and he glared at Joe.

UNDEAD PETS

"Five pounds, please," said the pet-shop owner.

Spiker was in such a rush to pay he dropped the coins on the floor. He bent down and scooped them up then counted them out. But one coin was missing — he was twenty pence short.

"Must have gone under the counter," he mumbled.

"Here," Joe dug in his pocket and handed over a coin.

"Thanks," Spiker muttered. Then he snatched up the box and turned to go.

"Wait!" said Joe. "My cousin lost his pet corn snake once…" He hoped the fib wouldn't show on his face. "I found it for him!"

"What? How?"

Joe shrugged. "You've just got to look in the right places."

"I've tried that—" Spiker stopped abruptly

when he realized he'd just admitted that he *had* lost a snake.

"I know loads of secret places that snakes hide," said Joe. "And there's always the flour trick!"

"The what?"

Before Joe could explain, a woman appeared in the shop.

"Bradley, there you are!" It was Mrs Piker — Spiker's mum. Joe giggled — no one at school ever called Spiker by his real name. "We've only got a few minutes left on the parking meter — come on!" She glanced at Joe and immediately recognized him from Spiker's class. "Joe, isn't it?" she smiled. "Enjoying half-term?"

"Yes, thanks."

"Lovely. Well, we've got to go now. Come on, Bradley!"

"Can Joe come round to our house?" Spiker said suddenly.

UNDEAD PETS

"What?" Joe turned to look at Spiker.

Mrs Piker looked shocked, too. "Well, I…" she stuttered.

"Joe wants to see Harley's pets," Spiker said. "As I'm looking after them while he's away, maybe I could show Joe today."

Joe remembered now that Spiker had once done a school presentation about his brother's collection of exotic pets.

"Joe's thinking of getting a corn snake!" Spiker added. "Aren't you, Joe?"

"Er, yeah." Joe nodded, uncertainly.

"And he'd like to come and meet Thor!"

Joe wondered why Spiker didn't just say that he wanted Joe to come round and help look for his brother's lost snake… But then it hit Joe like a thwack on the head with a cricket ball. Mrs Piker didn't know the snake had escaped!

"You boys and your snakes," she sighed, shaking her head. "Why you can't just have a nice hamster or a rabbit, I'll never know!"

"Can he come?" Spiker asked. "After lunch?"

"I suppose so," Mrs Piker replied. "You'd better ask your dad, Joe. Is that him over there?"

CHAPTER SIX

"Weird!" said Toby as they pulled up outside Spiker's house a few hours later. "Why are you going to Spiker's house? You hate him!"

"I don't!" Joe felt his cheeks redden.

"It *is* a bit odd," added Dad. "I mean, you've never wanted to hang out with him before."

Flash, who was sitting on Joe's knee, gave a sudden squeak. "They're home!" He was looking at the Crawfords' car, which was now parked in the drive outside their house. "I want to see Bolt and Lightning!"

UNDEAD PETS

As Joe opened the car door, Flash jumped off his knee, scrambled out and raced up the Crawfords' path, disappearing into the house.

"Can we go and see George?" asked Toby, undoing his seatbelt.

"No!" said Dad firmly. "You'll see George tomorrow at the party."

Toby refastened his belt. "S'pose."

Joe climbed out of the car and spotted Spiker waiting for him on his doorstep. Joe gulped. He felt like he was about to enter the dragon's lair.

"All right," mumbled Spiker. "Want to come upstairs?"

Spiker's house wasn't what Joe was expecting. In fact, it was just like his.

"That's my room," Spiker said, nodding to the first door on the landing. "Go in, if you want."

It was bigger than Joe's bedroom and much tidier. There were posters on the walls of snakes, lizards and spiders. In the corner was a small TV with a bean bag next to it and a pile of games stacked up. On top of the chest of drawers, Joe noticed several wooden models.

"Is that a lizard?" he asked, picking up the largest one.

"It's a komodo dragon," said Spiker. "I made it with my granddad. He's got an amazing workshop with loads of power tools."

Joe turned the model round to get a closer look.

"Careful! I spent ages on that." Spiker took it from Joe and put it back on his chest of drawers.

"Is that a rattlesnake?" Joe pointed to a poster above Spiker's bed.

"Yeah, it's an Eastern Diamondback Rattlesnake. That's the heaviest poisonous snake in America!"

"I've got a tree python's tooth at home," Joe said.

"Yeah, right!" Spiker rolled his eyes.

"No, really! My great-uncle Charlie got bitten by it when he was trekking in the rainforest in Australia! He brought the tooth back as a present for me."

Spiker shook his head. "Don't believe you."

"It's true – you can come round and see it if you want."

"Yeah?"

Joe nodded. Then he realized that he'd just invited his least favourite boy in the whole school round to his house. Working together to catch the snake was one thing, but hanging out together was another matter!

"Cool! A tarantula!" Joe said, pointing to another poster to change the subject.

"Yeah! Harley's got a real one. Do you want to see it?"

Joe followed Spiker back on to the landing.

"We've got to wash our hands first," Spiker said.

"What?" Joe asked, frowning.

"The bathroom's here. We shouldn't bring germs into the room," Spiker explained.

Joe looked at Spiker to figure out whether he was joking, but he was deadly serious.

They both washed their hands and then Spiker led the way to Harley's room.

It was a bit like a jungle. The curtains were

almost closed and the tank lights gave the room a greeny-yellow glow.

"Don't touch anything," hissed Spiker. "Harley's got everything fixed at the right temperature. All these creatures are very delicate!" Spiker crouched down by a plastic tank that contained an enormous hairy tarantula. "This is Zena," he said. "She's awesome, isn't she! Want to hold her?"

Joe hesitated. He didn't want Spiker to think he was a wimp, but didn't tarantulas bite?

"Ha! Only joking," smirked Spiker.

Joe tried not to look too relieved. "Does she bite?"

"Nah…"

Joe looked round at the other tanks. In one, a small spotty lizard was staring out at them.

"That's a leopard gecko," Spiker told Joe. "There are two of them in there, but the other one's shy. And that's Cheese next door…"

UNDEAD PETS

"Cheese?" Joe peered into the next tank.

"Yeah, his mate's called Pickle."

Joe smiled. "Is he a turtle?"

"No, he's a terrapin. Want to hold him?"

This time he wasn't joking.

"Remember, be careful!" growled Spiker. "Look, I'll show you…" He picked the terrapin up out of the tank. "You support him under his body like this."

He handed the terrapin to Joe, watching him like a hawk. "If you drop him, he'll die." Spiker glared menacingly at Joe. "And so will you!"

"He's amazing!" said Joe, peering at the tiny creature in his hand. "How do you know so much about all these animals?"

Spiker put the terrapin back in the tank. "Harley works at the Reptile Rescue Group in town. They rehome reptiles and amphibians."

"What do you mean?" Joe asked.

Spiker looked at Joe as if he was a moron. "They save abandoned pets! Some people don't want them when they get bigger. Or they don't look after them properly. So Reptile Rescue finds them new homes. Most of Harley's creatures come from there. He's just looking after them till they find permanent homes."

Joe looked around. It was strange to think these cool creatures were all unwanted pets.

"I'm gonna help the rescue group, too, when I'm old enough," Spiker said proudly.

"So what happened to Thor?" Joe asked.

Spiker looked embarrassed. "Harley's away for a few days on a training course. Me and Dad are looking after the animals for him. It's pretty easy. I can manage most of them myself. But I'm not allowed to touch the snakes without Dad."

"Then how did Thor escape?"

Spiker shrugged. "Thor's my favourite.

I only had him out for five minutes. I must have forgotten to put the brick on the lid of his vivarium when I put him back."

"And he pushed his way out?" asked Joe.

"Don't tell my parents! They'll never let me get a snake of my own if they find out!"

"Haven't they noticed?"

"No. Mum doesn't like the reptiles so she never comes in here and Dad trusts me. The snakes don't need to be fed every day…"

Joe nodded. He remembered reading that on the internet.

"Most of the time Dad just pops his head in and checks the sheet." Spiker pointed to a clipboard lying on the bed. "Harley makes me tick a feeding and care sheet for them all." Spiker frowned. "Anyway, we're gonna find Thor, aren't we! We've got to," growled Spiker, "or Harley will kill me!"

CHAPTER SEVEN

"Joe, Joe!"

Flash had appeared in Harley's bedroom. "You've got to come and look for the snake. I can smell it, but I can't see it!"

Suddenly Flash froze. He glanced round at all the strange creatures in the room then threw himself at Joe's feet, shaking like a jelly. "What is this place? It's horrible!" Perfumed bubbles exploded out of Flash's nose.

Spiker sniffed the air and looked at Joe suspiciously.

Joe coughed. "Should we start searching for Thor now?" he said to Spiker. "I bet there are loads of places a snake could hide in here."

Flash gave an indignant snort. "The snake's not in here!" He head-butted Joe's ankle angrily. "The snake's next door!"

"Let's wash our hands again, then we'll start looking," said Spiker.

"What?" Joe frowned. "But we just washed them!"

"But we touched the terrapin. They can spread salmonella," Spiker replied.

Spiker is never this sensible at school! Joe thought.

"You go first," said Spiker. "I've got to check the terrapins' tank to make sure the lid is on properly."

Flash followed Joe into the bathroom. "You've got to come and find that snake! Now!"

Joe turned on the tap then scooped Flash

up. "Listen, Flash," he whispered. "Thor might have come back here again – he could be in Spiker's house now. We're going to look for him!"

"The snake is *not* here," Flash snorted. "It's next door!"

"Well, maybe I can find out how he got next door and then put some food down to tempt him back. That's what the pet- shop man told Spiker to do. It's worth a try!"

For the next hour they looked everywhere. Luckily Spiker's mum was too busy gardening to notice.

"Check the bin!" said Joe as they peered inside the kitchen cupboards. "And round the back of the fridge, too. The motor makes it warm."

"It's not there!" grumbled Flash from Joe's pocket. "I've told you – the snake's next door!"

"Where did you find your cousin's snake?" asked Spiker.

Joe blushed. He hated fibbing. "It was inside the airing cupboard," he said, remembering where the girl in the shop had found her boa constrictor.

"Right, we'll look there, too!"

Ten minutes later they were back upstairs in Harley's room.

"Nothing," groaned Spiker. "Harley's going to go ballistic!"

Joe didn't reply. He was on his hands and knees, peering behind Thor's vivarium. He could see a large crack in the skirting board. He stood up and patted the wall. "This leads through to next door, doesn't it?"

Spiker nodded.

"What if Thor crawled through the gap

behind the tank? Maybe he got through to the house next door."

"Ha!" scoffed Spiker. "I think I'd have heard if a snake had appeared in the Crawfords' house!"

"It has, it has!" squealed Flash.

"Yeah," said Joe. "But what if he's found somewhere cosy to hide? Maybe they don't know."

"Mum would go crazy!" Spiker replied.

"Fetch some snake food," said Joe, "and leave it by this crack. Maybe the smell will make Thor come back. When did you last feed him?"

"A few days ago. So he'll be getting hungry," said Spiker. "I'll go and fetch some dead mice to put out for him."

"Dead mice!" squeaked Flash. Joe's pocket began to quake.

"AHHHHH!" Joe sat bolt upright in the darkness.

"What is it, Joe?" Flash poked his head out from under the bedsheet.

"SNAKES!" spluttered Joe. "EVERYWHERE!"

Flash gave a squeal and dived back under the covers.

"Joe?" His bedroom light went on. Dad stood in the doorway.

Joe blinked a few times, then realized he'd been dreaming.

Undead Pets

After spending the afternoon at Spiker's house, all he'd been able to think about was

snakes! Now he was dreaming about them, too.

"Snakes," Joe said, suddenly feeling a bit silly. "They were everywhere! Under the floorboards, popping out of the taps, in the toilet…"

"I think you've been spending too much time with Spiker and his scary pets!" said Dad.

"They're not scary – they're amazing, really…"

"I'll take your word for it, Joe! Goodnight!" Dad turned off the light and shut the door.

"You can come out now!" whispered Joe.

Flash gave a squeak. "Not until the snakes have gone!"

"There weren't any snakes. I was just dreaming."

Flash scrabbled up. "Are you sure? Poor Bolt and Lightning – I wonder if they've seen the snake. They'll be terrified! And what if it's already eaten them?" grumbled Flash.

"Thor's probably back in Harley's room by now," said Joe. "You'll be gone by the morning!"

"What?"

"Well," mumbled Joe sleepily. "If Thor goes home, your problems will be solved." *And I'll get my bed back to myself*, he thought with a smile.

But when morning came, Flash was still there.

"I don't want to go to the dentist today!" wailed Toby, who was sitting at the kitchen table, squishing the last bits of his breakfast cereal with the back of his spoon. "Why do we have to go? It's the holidays!"

Mum ignored him. "Hurry up with your breakfast, Joe," she said, picking up Toby's bowl and putting it in the sink. "And Toby, go and brush your teeth." Then she turned to Dad. "Don't forget you're dropping Toby at George's party this afternoon – I've got clients until five o'clock. Are you sure you don't want to go, Joe?"

"What?" Joe was thinking about snakes again.

"The party – at George and Erin's house?"

Joe frowned. Maybe he *should* go. To see if he could spot the snake…

"Don't you want to see Doctor Franken-Bubble?" asked Toby, prodding Joe's arm. "The monster party's going to be so exciting!"

Yeah, thought Joe, *especially if an enormous snake shows up!*

CHAPTER EIGHT

The dentist's waiting room was large and airy with huge squishy sofas. Joe recognized a few kids from school waiting with their parents. Toby and a girl from his class were peering at a cabinet full of toothbrushes for sale.

"I want that one!" Toby said, pointing to a green brush with a monster's head on the end. "Or the troll one. It's really cool!"

"Maybe afterwards," said Mum, wiping her nose with a tissue. Her allergies were bothering her again, thanks to Flash's fur. She blew her nose noisily. "It's us next!"

At that moment the dental nurse appeared. "Joe and Toby Edmunds. Follow me."

Joe slipped off his coat with Flash inside the pocket. "Wait here!" he whispered, laying it on the back of the sofa next to Toby's fleece.

Flash gave an impatient snort.

The nurse led them into the consulting room.

"Who's going first?" asked Mr Ridge, the dentist.

"Joe!" squeaked Toby, who'd spotted the dentist's shiny instruments lined up on a stand next to the big black chair. "Can I go for a wee?"

Mum sighed. "Can't you wait?"

Toby made a face. "I'm desperate!"

"Come on then." Mum took his hand. "I'll show you where it is."

Joe climbed into the chair.

"If you could just put these glasses on, then

sit back," said the nurse.

Joe blinked under the bright lights.

"Open wide," said Mr Ridge.

As he began working through Joe's teeth, tapping, prodding and checking each in turn, Joe heard a noise by the door. It was the sound of small scratchy footsteps.

"Joe?" squeaked Flash. "JOE! What's that man doing to you? Is he the vet?"

Joe groaned. He was helpless – he couldn't move, he couldn't speak, there was no way he could tell Flash what was happening. He wriggled anxiously.

Mr Ridge stopped for a moment. "Everything OK, Joe? Does it hurt there?"

Joe shook his head.

"What's he doing?" squeaked Flash.

Joe gripped the chair with frustration. Why hadn't Flash stayed in the waiting room!

"Is he hurting you?" Flash squealed.

Joe turned his head slightly, trying to catch a glimpse of Flash and show him he was fine.

"It's OK, Joe," soothed the dentist. "We're nearly finished. Nothing to worry about…"

"Joe? Joe? Speak to me!" Flash was jumping up and down, flowery bubbles erupting from his nose.

At that moment, Mum and Toby came back. Mum let out a sudden sneeze!

Joe jumped and Mr Ridge stepped back, bumping into the stand holding his equipment.

It wobbled and then…

"Look out!" called the nurse, as the instruments clattered down to the floor.

"Oops!" giggled Toby. "Does that mean I miss my turn?"

"I'm so, so sorry," Mum kept saying as she made their next appointment.

The receptionist smiled patiently. "It wasn't your fault, Mrs Edmunds."

Mum blew her nose. "My allergies have been terrible lately!"

Joe felt his face turn red. He shoved Flash even deeper into his coat pocket.

"Hey!" the guinea pig squeaked. "I can't breathe!"

You don't need to! thought Joe. *You're already dead!*

"Look!" Toby nudged Joe. "It's Spiker!"

Joe glanced up. It *was* Spiker.

"All right, Joe!" Spiker said.

"What are you doing here?" Joe asked.

"Same as you!" Spiker grinned.

"I'll just tell them we're here," Mrs Piker said. "Hello again, Joe. We seem to be seeing rather a lot of you!" She smiled and headed to the reception desk.

Toby had spotted the toothbrushes again. "Mum! Can I have the troll one?"

"Any sign of Thor?" Joe whispered to Spiker.

Spiker glanced over at Toby. "Nah," he muttered.

"There's still time," Joe said hopefully.

Spiker nodded. "He'll be starving by now!"

"What?" Flash poked his head out of Joe's pocket. "Did you hear that?" he squeaked. "The snake's starving and I know what he'll want for dinner – fresh guinea pig, that's what!"

"I'm going to a party today," said Toby, coming over to Joe and Spiker.

"Great!" said Spiker.

"There's going to be loads of awesome food. Pizza, sausages, hot dogs… I love hot dogs!"

Joe was just about to tell Toby to put a sock in it when a horrible thought wriggled into his brain. What if Thor was attracted to the party food instead of his snake grub? Did snakes eat sausages?

"It's at George's house," went on Toby. "Next door to you! And there's going to be loads of kids and games and prizes. And Doctor Franken-Bubble!"

"What?" Spiker was listening now. "George is having a party? A big one?"

Toby nodded. "Do you want to go?"

"No, thanks!" Spiker said. Then he turned to Joe and dropped his voice to a whisper, so only Joe could hear. "If Thor is in the Crawfords' house, he'll be terrified of the noise. Snakes get stressed!"

"What?" Joe looked at Spiker.

"Snakes are sensitive creatures!" Spiker hissed.

"Ha!" snorted Flash. "Sensitive creatures – as if! More like guinea-pig gobbling slithery slime balls!"

"And we're gonna play pass-the-parcel and have a treasure hunt," Toby added.

Spiker's eyes narrowed. "Little kids are terrible round snakes." He scowled at Toby. "They're too rough and noisy!"

Joe hadn't really thought about the snake's

feelings in all this. After all, it was a pet, too. "We've got to find Thor!" he said quietly.

"How?" Spiker demanded.

"I'll go to the party," said Joe.

"Oh, what a dreadful thing to have happened…"

Mum was on the phone to Mrs Crawford. She was asking if it would be all right for Joe to go to the party. When he'd told her he'd changed his mind, she'd nearly crashed the car on to the pavement! He'd said that he would actually like to see the bubble man.

"Oh, yes," Mum was saying to Mrs Crawford. "I can imagine Erin and George must have been devastated."

"What is it?" Toby looked at Joe across the lunch table.

Joe shrugged.

"Yes," Mum went on. "He was so cute.

That lovely squeaking noise he made… Such a shame you've lost him."

Joe gulped. It sounded like another guinea pig had died!

"Oh dear," Mum added, nodding. She was quiet for a while, then after a few moments, she said, "Thanks so much, the boys can't wait!"

Mum ended the phone call and looked at Joe and Toby with a glum expression on her face. "I'm really sorry, boys, but I'm afraid I've got some sad news."

"What?" Toby looked terrified. "The party's not cancelled, is it?"

"No, Carol's looking forward to seeing you both this afternoon. But I'm afraid one of Erin and George's guinea pigs has died."

"NO!" squealed Flash, who was snuffling about under the table next to Joe's feet. "The snake's got them!"

Joe felt his throat go tight. He'd failed in

his mission. One of the guinea pigs had been gobbled up!

"Which one?" asked Toby, his voice a bit quivery.

"Flash!" said Mum. "I'm really sorry."

"Who? What? Me?" From under the table, Flash gave a shocked squeak.

UNDEAD PETS

Of course! Joe sighed with relief. Mrs Crawford was telling Mum about Flash's tragic end in the washing machine. Joe had forgotten that no one else knew what had happened to Flash after they'd left the Crawfords' house.

He tried not to smile. If only Mum and Toby knew that, at that very moment, Flash was sitting on the floor nibbling Toby's lunch crumbs!

"That's so sad," said Toby. His lip was trembling. "I liked Flash best!"

Flash puffed up his chest proudly.

"What are you going to wear to the party, Joe?" asked Mum, trying to change the subject.

"It's a monster party," said Toby, still looking tearful. "I'm going as a troll."

Joe looked desperately at Mum. "I don't have to dress up, do I?"

Mum smiled and shook her head. "Don't worry, Joe. You can wear what you like!"

CHAPTER NINE

A few hours later, Dad, Joe and Toby were on the Crawfords' doorstep. There were balloons tied to the letterbox and a big "HAPPY BIRTHDAY" banner taped across the front door. Flash had already scrambled out of Joe's rucksack and vanished into the house.

Through the front window they could see a crowd of kids dancing round the living room. The sound of laughter and shrieking and loud music boomed out.

"Do you think the present will be OK?" asked

Dad, ringing the bell again. "Maybe guinea-pig toys aren't the best thing to give a boy whose pet has just died!"

Toby hugged the brightly wrapped box tightly. "He's still got Bolt and Lightning!"

Not for much longer if I don't find that snake, thought Joe.

"Toby! Joe!" The door burst open and George stood there, wearing a Frankenstein costume. He had a pretend bolt through his neck and scars painted on his face. "We're playing musical statues!"

HAPPY BIRTHDAY

"Hi, Joe," said Erin, appearing behind Toby. She was dressed as a zombie – her hair messy, her raggedy dress covered in red paint. "Want to come through to the kitchen – away from the little kids?"

"Hey!" George made a cross face, then darted off. "Quick, Toby!" he yelled. "In the living room."

"Goodbye then, boys! Have fun." Joe's dad turned and headed towards the car.

"Do you want some lemonade, Joe?" asked Erin. "Watch out!" she yelped as three small monsters zoomed past them, spilling handfuls of cheese puffs everywhere.

"Wow!" Joe said, when he saw the kitchen.

Every surface was covered with food and right in the middle was a giant chocolate monster cake!

"Help yourself to some snacks," Erin said.

As Joe scooped up a handful of crisps, Erin

poured some lemonade into two paper cups.

"I'm laying out the treasure-hunt clues. You can help me if you like."

"Uh-huh," mumbled Joe, but he wasn't listening. He was peering behind the fridge. Was Thor there?

"What are you doing?" Erin gave him a funny look.

"Nothing," said Joe. "I think we've got the same fridge as you…" he added.

"Did your mum tell you what happened to Flash?"

Joe nodded.

"I miss him!" Erin sniffed.

Joe shuffled his feet uncomfortably. He never knew what to say when people were upset.

"JOE!" Flash burst into the room. "The guinea pigs have gone. They're not in their hutch!"

"Where are they?" Joe said, realizing too

late that he had spoken to Flash out loud.

"Who?" Erin frowned.

"Er, I mean, where are the other guinea pigs?" asked Joe.

"Outside in their run. Mum thought it would be safer for them with all the little kids in the house."

"Phew!" said Flash. "Right, let's start looking for the snake." He vanished back through the kitchen door.

"Where are you going to hide the clues?" Joe asked Erin, taking a quick look in the kitchen bin, just in case Thor had snuck inside.

"I've done most of them. There's just a few we need to put upstairs." Erin picked up some bits of paper and sticky tape and headed for the door. "Follow me!"

As soon as her back was turned, Joe quickly opened a couple of kitchen cupboards and peered inside.

"Joe?" Erin was watching him.

"Sorry! I like your cupboard doors. They … don't creak when you open them." He wiggled them a bit. "See? Ours creak all the time!"

"Oh, right," said Erin, looking at him as though he was mad. "Anyway, come on."

For the next ten minutes Joe helped Erin with the clues, keeping an eye out for the snake the whole time. He checked inside the laundry basket, in the airing cupboard, under the beds…

"Come on," Erin called from the bathroom.

As Joe crossed the landing, Flash zoomed out through a door. "Seen it?" he squeaked.

Joe shook his head.

"Me neither. Hurry, Joe – this is our only chance!" And he scuttled off again, vanishing through another door.

Inside the bathroom, Joe noticed a tall cupboard with a latch at the top. At the bottom of it was a small hole next to the skirting board. Joe peered at it. Was it big enough for a snake to squeeze through? "What's in there?"

"That's the door to the loft," said Erin, taping the last clue to the shampoo bottles.

"Can I look inside?"

"No, Dad doesn't like us playing up there. It's not safe – there are no proper floorboards."

Joe looked at the hole again and then up at the ceiling. What if that was the way Thor had got into the house? Maybe he'd wriggled over from Spiker's loft into the Crawfords' house? Maybe he was up there now!

Joe thought quickly. "Erin, I just need to use the toilet."

After she'd left the bathroom, Joe stood on tiptoes and unhooked the latch on the door that led to the attic.

"Joe? What is it?" Flash had appeared through the bathroom door. "Have you found something?"

"I'm not sure…" Joe opened the door. Inside was a narrow cupboard with a ladder leading up to the attic. There was a flashlight on the ground.

"Pick me up, Joe!"

With Flash clinging to his shoulder and the torch stuffed down his belt, Joe began climbing the ladder.

"Hey!" Joe yelped, halfway up. "Don't hold on so tight. It hurts!"

"I can't help it!" squeaked Flash. "I'm nervous.

UNDEAD PETS

What if it's up there?"

"Well, it can't hurt you. You're dead already!" Joe replied.

But he was thinking the same thing. He'd never come eyeball to eyeball with a snake before. Even if Thor wasn't dangerous to humans, Joe still didn't like the idea of creeping up on him!

Cautiously, Joe eased his head up through the hole. He turned on the torch and flashed it around.

"Nothing." He breathed a sigh of relief. "Just some spiders and a few bits of old junk!"

"Hey!" Joe felt a tug on his leg. He turned and bumped his head. "Ow!"

"What are you doing? I heard you banging around in there!" Erin was staring up at him. "Dad will go bonkers if he sees you!"

UNDEAD PETS

Joe floundered, desperately trying to think of a fib.

"Don't tell me. You want to know if our attic is as dusty as yours!" Erin said sarcastically.

Joe flicked the torch off and clambered down.

"Tell her, Joe. Erin will understand. She's nice," said Flash.

Joe hesitated, then he sighed and said, "I'm looking for a snake."

"What?" Erin rolled her eyes. "Very funny!"

"It's true! It escaped from Spiker's house — you know, the boy next door. It's a corn snake called Thor. Me and Spiker think it's come through the wall into your house."

"Awesome!" Erin breathed.

"Aren't you freaked out?"

Erin shook her head. "I love snakes!"

"How could she!" Flash squeaked indignantly.

"It's just that, I thought maybe you wouldn't want it near the guinea pigs…"

Erin's face fell. "Do snakes eat guinea pigs?"

"Well, they eat mice," said Joe.

"Oh!" Erin looked worried. "Where could it be?" She glanced round the bathroom.

"I've looked everywhere," sighed Joe. "I thought the attic was a good bet but it's probably too cold up there. Snakes like the warm." Joe flicked some dust and cobwebs off his shirt. "I'm not sure where to look next."

Erin frowned. "I don't understand why we haven't seen it. Mum and Dad have been cleaning for days for George's party. How come they didn't spot it?"

Joe shrugged.

"Maybe it's gone home again," said Erin.

"We could check with Spiker," Joe suggested.

Just then there was a loud cheer from the

back garden, followed by excited shrieks.

Erin flipped open the bathroom window and peered out. "It's Doctor Franken-Bubble!"

Joe looked over her shoulder. A crazy-looking man with a green wig, a white lab coat and bright red trousers was standing in the middle of the lawn with a bubble blower spitting out hundreds of bubbles.

"ERIN! JOE!"

"That's Mum," said Erin. "Come on, we'd better go down."

CHAPTER TEN

By the time Joe and Erin got outside, the lawn was a sea of bubbles. George and his friends were racing around after them.

"Look, Joe!" shouted Toby. "They're amazing!"

"I can see Lightning and Bolt!" squeaked Flash. "Put me down, Joe!"

The guinea pigs were on the other side of the garden in their run.

"I'm going to check on them," Flash said.

Joe looked round the garden. Maybe Thor was

out here somewhere, soaking up the sunshine!

Just then, there was a squeal of excitement from the children as Doctor Franken-Bubble picked up an enormous hoop, dipped it in a paddling pool full of gloopy bubble mixture, and wafted it above his head, making the most humongous bubble Joe had ever seen! "In a moment, I'll show you how to put a boy inside a bubble!" shouted Doctor Franken-Bubble.

"But first, let's turn up the bubble machine!"

Joe spotted Spiker waving to him from across the garden fence.

"Did you find Thor?" Spiker demanded.

Before Joe could answer, Erin appeared.

"We've looked everywhere," she said. "But there's no sign of your snake!"

Spiker glared at Joe. "Did you tell her?"

"It's OK. I like snakes." Erin smiled.

"Really?" Spiker's face softened slightly. Then his frown came back. "We've got to find him! Harley's on his way home. He's just called Mum – he's coming back early. If Thor's not in his tank, I'll be dogfood!"

"JOE! JOE!" Flash came hurtling over. "Joe! Stop them!" he squeaked. "They're taking the guinea pigs inside!"

Joe turned. Doctor Franken-Bubble was having a break. He was chatting to Erin's mum and dad, with a mug of tea in his hand, while the kids chased after bubbles from his automatic bubble machine.

But that wasn't what was upsetting Flash.

"Look!" he squealed.

A small group of children were disappearing indoors. George and Toby were among them – and they had Bolt and Lightning in their arms!

"What are they doing?" said Erin. "Mum told George not to get the guinea pigs out when there are so many kids about. They'll be terrified!"

"The obstacle course," groaned Joe. "Toby was going on about it in the car. I bet he's asked George to set it up again."

"The snake will get them!" squealed Flash.

"We'd better stop them." Erin turned to Spiker. "Want to come and look for the snake?"

Spiker nodded. He climbed over the fence. Joe scooped up Flash and shoved him into his pocket. They raced across the lawn.

As they reached the house, Joe heard a shriek from inside. It sounded like Toby!

The kitchen was in chaos.

"They've escaped!" Toby was yelling.

George was crying.

"What happened?" Erin demanded. "Where are the guinea pigs?"

"They got scared and ran off!" he wailed.

"Found one!" shouted a girl from the living room.

UNDEAD PETS

Erin went off to see.

"It's Lightning!" she called back a moment later. "No sign of Bolt, though."

George began crying even more.

"Stop it, you're making too much noise!" growled Spiker. "Snakes hate noise," he added in a whisper to Joe.

Joe glared at Spiker. His pet wasn't the only one in danger. What if the snake had got the guinea pig!

"I'm going to look for Thor," said Spiker, heading upstairs.

"What about Bolt?" squeaked Flash. "Find him, Joe!"

"Check the hall!" shouted Erin from the living room. "See if Bolt's in amongst the shoes."

Joe raced over to the shoe basket and began rummaging inside…

Nothing! He groaned. Then he spotted a sports bag by the front door. He pulled it open. *Someone's sweaty sports kit, but no guinea pig!*

"Any luck?" shouted Erin from the living room.

"Do something, Joe," squeaked Flash. "We have to save Bolt! He could be getting gobbled up right now!"

Joe looked around desperately. Where would a panicking guinea pig go? Then suddenly he had an idea. He leaned in close to Flash.

"Where would you hide in the house if you were scared?"

"What?" Flash stopped squeaking and looked at Joe.

"Where would you hide? That's where Bolt will be!"

Flash twitched his nose. "Under the floorboards in the dining room!"

"What?"

"There's a gap behind the bookcase. I went there once when I escaped out of my hutch," Flash squeaked.

Joe dashed into the dining room. He spotted the bookcase immediately.

"Bolt?" he called, bending down to look.

"See," said Flash. "There's a gap behind it."

Joe peered round and saw a half-broken floorboard, with a gap big enough for a guinea pig to hide in. He tugged at it with his hands and then gasped.

An orange snake's head popped out, its tongue flicking as it tasted the air.

Flash gave a loud squeal and darted away.

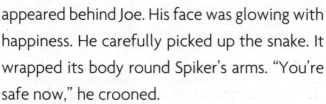

"Thor!" Joe breathed.

"You found him!" Spiker appeared behind Joe. His face was glowing with happiness. He carefully picked up the snake. It wrapped its body round Spiker's arms. "You're safe now," he crooned.

"Good job we got him," Joe said. "He might have gobbled up Bolt!"

Spiker rolled his eyes. "Thor prefers dead mice!"

"Wow!" Erin appeared next to them. "He's awesome!"

"Where's Bolt?" asked Joe.

"He was in the kitchen, hiding behind the vegetable rack. George's getting a telling-off from Mum!" Erin giggled. She pointed to the snake. "Can I hold him?"

"He's a bit scared of strangers," said Spiker.

"WHAT'S GOING ON IN HERE?" Erin's mum stood in the doorway. She blinked at the snake as though she couldn't believe her eyes.

"This is Spiker from next door and his pet snake, Thor," said Erin calmly. "I asked Spiker to bring him round to show George, as a special treat for his birthday."

"That's very kind of you … Spiker," Mrs Crawford said. "But maybe it would be better when there's less chaos!"

"MUM!" George was calling from the hall.

As Mrs Crawford went out, Spiker smiled at Erin. "Thanks for not telling."

Erin shrugged. "Want me to help you take the snake home?"

"Sure!" said Spiker. "Have you got a box?"

"Yeah, I think so. There's a shoebox in my room. Come on!"

Joe went to follow them, but just then he heard a small squeak. Flash was sitting on the ledge next to the open window.

"Bye, Joe!"

"What? Are you going already?"

Flash smiled at Joe and a stream of bubbles popped out of his mouth. "Thanks for everything."

And with that, he vanished, leaving nothing but a few bubbles floating round the room.

UNDEAD PETS

"Hey, Joe!" Toby stuck his head into the room. "Doctor Franken-Bubble's about to make square bubbles. Come and see!"

Joe grinned and turned to go when suddenly he heard a strange high-pitched whine coming from behind the armchair.

"Who's there?" Joe said